POLLY - MAIL ORDER BRIDE

THE CHRISTMAS BRIDES OF JEFFERSON CITY

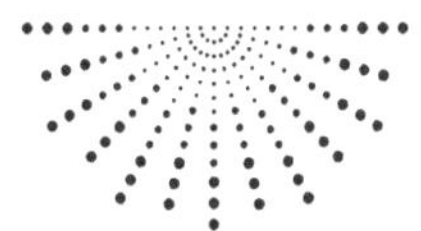

INDIANA WAKE

BELLE FIFFER

The Christmas Brides of Jefferson City

Everything is in bloom in Jefferson City at the beginning of summer but the Mayor has only one thing on his mind. He wants to find wives for his sons by Christmas!

Mayor Arnold Foster is a dominant man that not many want to cross. When he demands that Pastor Thomas Brooks find Mail Order Brides for all *Six* of his sons the good pastor is reluctant. The Mayor will not be thwarted and resorts to threats. Pastor Brooks reluctantly agrees, knowing that he is the better person to take care of the women than whomever the mayor would get next.

Mayor Foster's sons are in no hurry to marry, in fact, they are totally against anything their father could suggest. Six strong and stubborn men will not be easy to persuade.

Pastor Brooks must rely on his faith and strength of character to find the perfect women for the Foster men. He is determined to find matches that will bring love and peace into all the lives of those involved.

Will Pastor Brooks succeed in bringing love to Jefferson City just in time for Christmas?

The books in this series each tell a complete story of one couple

The Christmas Brides of Jefferson City

Nicola

Amy

Polly

Shelley

Anne

Jacira

Tracy

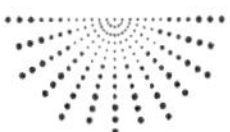

CHAPTER ONE

"How are you holding up?"

Sheriff Chris Foster pressed a hand to his stomach and winced. His color had returned a little. At least now he wasn't completely gray and sweating.

"I'll live. Ernest said it didn't hit anything vital, but it's going to hurt like... well." Chris made a face. "James is refusing to let me go home at the moment."

"As he should." Morgan folded his arms as he sat beside his brother's bed. "You could've died."

Chris snorted.

"I'm tougher than that."

"Tell that to Ernest. He's still not got much color back in his face. You look better than he does right now."

"I didn't ask to get stabbed," Chris protested.

Morgan didn't respond. He was still reeling from the fact his younger brother, easily the toughest out of all of them, had ended up having someone get the better of him. He had been stabbed trying to rescue Amy from her father, who was hell-bent on taking her back home to force her into marriage. That all ended when Dominic Growcott stabbed Chris and ran for the hills.

He was lucky Chris didn't die; otherwise, Morgan would be going after him for murder. And it would be Morgan's job to find him. No one else was taking on this task. Morgan wanted to be the one who dragged Growcott back to face his crimes. They weren't the worst that Morgan had encountered, but this time it was personal.

"I wish I could go after him myself." Chris winced as he slumped back onto the pillows. "But I know as soon as I get up from here, I'll be sent back to bed."

"I know. James and Amy have already told me that you're not leaving here for at least a week."

"What about my job? Jefferson City needs a sheriff."

Morgan rolled his eyes.

"I'm sure your deputies can manage without you. They're not halfwits."

"Even so…"

"Calm yourself, brother, or you're going to bust your stitches." Morgan held up a hand as Chris started to protest. "My job is also hunting down these animals. I can handle it."

"I know you can." Chris closed his eyes for a brief moment. "But can you go after one who hasn't got a bounty on their head?"

"I don't need the bounty. He tried to kill a lawman. That's enough for anyone to go after him."

Morgan was happy to do this for free. He could be at odds with his family, but the moment someone hurt one of his brothers, he was going to be at the front of it all to get his own back. No one harmed his brothers and got away with it.

At least Growcott would be easy enough to overpower. James had shot him, that had to slow him down. The closest doctor for five miles was Ernest, and Growcott was certainly not going to go there when he had just tried to kill the doctor's brother.

"Just be careful, he won't be as easy as you might think," Chris said. "That man is single-minded, and he knows what he wants."

"How is that not easy? It makes him predictable"

"I... I... just be careful." Morgan grunted.

"I think you need some more laudanum. It's wearing off."

"It makes me feel groggy."

"And it also makes you talk normally without sounding nonsensical." Morgan sat forward. "Do you think he's going to come back and get his daughter again?"

"I know he will. He's that desperate for her. I reckon he got himself into such a mess she is his only way out of it. What a joke, selling his daughter to pay his debts!"

Morgan knew that much. Polly had spoken to him about Amy's predicament when Amy was cagey about her reasons for coming here. Her father was a gambler and he chose money over everything else. He loved to play cards or dice whenever he could to the point where he had lost his job. Amy's mother had died and her inheritance from her wealthy family went straight to Growcott, despite her family's objections. That money had vanished within months. Then Growcott had decided to use Amy as a pawn, one of his creditors suggesting that he could wipe out all of Growcott's debts if he gave Amy to him as his wife. Naturally, Amy had objected and violently opposed it, but her father refused to listen. As long as it got him back to where he wanted, he didn't care.

That was why Amy had run away. She had made sure that nobody would be able to tell her father where she had gone, telling only a select few. But Growcott had found out anyway, and now he was in Jefferson City planning on taking her back. Months after the deal had been made, it was still surprisingly in effect. Growcott had acted like a madman, not willing to sit down and talk it out. If he had come like that, then things might have turned out better.

Morgan was sure that the only person Growcott loved was himself. He didn't love his daughter if he was willing to give her over to a creditor. In Morgan's mind, Amy was right to leave. Growcott was clearly of a different opinion.

Now he had gotten himself into more trouble. It was bad enough that he went after someone Morgan liked, she was also the object of his brother James's affections. James would not have let Amy go anywhere, and he made a point of proving it.

At least he had finally confessed to Amy how he felt before he lost her, otherwise, that would be another Foster brother with a broken heart. Morgan knew they didn't need any more of them.

"And I thought our father was bad," Morgan muttered.

Chris snorted, followed by a slight groan.

"Father never sold us off for money. Who knows if he would have... after all, he never needed to. Still, Father and Growcott are as bad as each other, that much is undeniable."

Morgan couldn't agree more about that comment.

Arnold Foster was a man who wouldn't listen unless it was for his own means. He didn't even believe that his father loved his sons anymore. They were just a means to an end. It had to be his way or he threw a tantrum.

Like getting all of his sons married by Christmas Day because he wanted to show that he had a big happy family. Morgan wanted to throttle his father for trying to force them into something none of them wanted. Now it was appearing to him that his brothers were buckling. Matthew's nanny had captured his heart, James had finally confessed his love to his housekeeper, and Morgan had witnessed Ernest and Adam soften as well.

He wouldn't soften. Even if there was a good reason to soften not far away.

"By the way, James got word from Father a short while ago." Morgan rubbed his hand over his face. "Father says he's shocked at what's happening and denied having pointed Growcott in Amy's direction."

Chris rolled his eyes.

"Of course, he would. Because then he would be

admitting to having a minor part in my assault. We probably never will know if he had a role in this. He loves the drama, and he doesn't reveal anything unless it benefits him."

"Which I find annoying, seeing as he was aiming at getting James married and Amy was the obvious choice."

"As I said, he loves drama, and he's not going to be the one going after Growcott."

Morgan grunted.

"Maybe he should. Then he'll see what we have to deal with."

"As if you'll get him out from behind his desk." Chris's mouth twitched with a smile. "Did you know James has asked Amy to marry him?"

"I know. James told me when I arrived just now." Morgan sat back and stared at the ceiling. "He and Matthew have gone mad."

"Matthew's engaged as well?"

"He proposed to Nicola last night. I heard about it this morning."

Chris arched an eyebrow. Then he shook his head with a slight chuckle.

"Sounds like our old man's going to get his wish about his children getting married at Christmas."

"Not with everyone. It won't happen."

"You're that determined to resist, are you?"

"Aren't you?"

Chris made a growling sound and looked away. But Morgan saw him absently rub his fingers over the part of his finger where his wedding ring would have been.

"Remember what happened last Christmas? I'm not going to go through that again."

Morgan couldn't blame him for that. Chris had meant to be married the previous Christmas to Olivia, a pretty girl who had been in love with Chris since she was barely walking. Chris had finally returned her feelings after years of dancing around each other. Morgan had thought the two of them were a good match. Until Olivia didn't turn up to her wedding day because she had met someone else and had gone to marry him instead. Chris had been devastated, breaking down as soon as he was away from the pitying looks. Morgan had seen his brother become a shadow of his former self and withdraw from everyone, even his brothers. It took the other brothers nearly six months to get Chris back to any resemblance of what he had been, and even then, it was difficult to get him to open up. Chris just threw himself into his work.

Although Morgan was sure he had seen Chris soften towards a certain young mother. Anne Brough had come with the other women Pastor Thomas Brooks had brought to Jefferson City under Mayor Foster's orders, as women to be married off to his six sons. Like his brothers, Chris had objected to it and declared it wouldn't happen; he was still recovering from his former bride's betrayal. But Morgan had seen him around Anne, a widow with a three-year-old daughter, and had watched as he started smiling more. Especially when little Tamsin Brough started reaching for him, choosing to seek him out instead of her mother.

Morgan couldn't blame him for turning to mush over a child. Tamsin was an adorable little girl. Chris would certainly be a good father; he loved children. But Chris wasn't about to admit that he was softening his opinion about his father's choice to pair them off. Like Morgan, that would mean telling Arnold Foster that he had won.

But isn't that what you've been doing for the last six months? Haven't you been softening towards a lovely young lady who is only just a few feet away downstairs?

No, I haven't. And I won't.

Morgan felt like a liar as he argued with himself.

"Morgan?"

Chris was looking at him oddly. Morgan cleared his throat and shifted in his seat.

"Sorry, did you say something?"

Chris frowned. "I just asked, did you know that Polly is planning on hunting for Growcott herself?"

That caught Morgan off-guard. He stared. "She what? Why?"

"Because Amy's her friend, and Polly's very angry."

Morgan groaned. This was just what he needed. He wanted to go out first thing in the morning and hunt for Growcott without any distractions. If Polly went out on her own, Morgan was going to have to play nanny to her, and he didn't have time to deal with a woman with a fiery temper. And a fiery temper she certainly had. A smile came across his face. Morgan had to admire it, even if it was often directed at him. Then again, he did tend to goad Polly into it. He liked fire in a woman, and Polly had a lot of it. She was also a beautiful woman who could bake, in so many ways he couldn't fault her.

Except for being impulsive. This was not the type of job for a woman. Morgan knew that from personal experience. He had already lost someone he cared about working alongside him. He wasn't about to do it with Polly.

Did he care about her? Absolutely. And Morgan would make sure she stayed with her friend. The wilderness was not a place for Polly Brown.

"Thanks for warning me." Morgan rose to his feet. "But I'll handle this. I'll make sure she comes back."

"From what I've seen of her and what I've gathered since she arrived, you're going to have a fight on your hands. She's very stubborn."

"So am I." Morgan leaned over and squeezed his brother's shoulder. "You rest up. I don't want you collapsing again."

"This isn't as painful as last Christmas." Chris managed a small smile. "I can handle it."

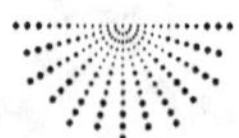

CHAPTER TWO

Polly stood at the end of her bed and looked over everything laid out in front of her. All of it seemed to be in order, and it was ready to be packed. She had arranged for a horse to be ready to go first thing in the morning. For a moment she glanced out the window. Should she set off now, to give the man who tried to kidnap her friend less of an advantage? It was very dark outside. Even her father would struggle to track in these conditions, for her it would be close to impossible. It was best to use the most natural light she could.

Which meant waiting until the morning. Only, Polly hated the wait. The man who went after his daughter, her friend, deserved to be taken in immediately. But her father's reasonings were right; she didn't know the lay of the land and in the dark, she would be helpless. Patience had to come into play, or she could end up losing Growcott. Even wounded, he would be able to put distance between Jefferson City and wherever he was planning to go.

A few thoughts flew through her mind, telling her that maybe she should leave this to a professional lawman. Morgan was a US Marshal; this was his job. He would be hunting Dominic Growcott, and Polly trusted him to find the man. Even so, she couldn't sit back and do nothing. She had promised Amy to look after her, and she hadn't done that. Amy was safe now, but Polly felt the need to atone. No one was going to stop her from going out there to find Growcott.

He could only hope he bled to death before she found him.

"I heard you're going to look for Growcott."

Polly spun around. Morgan was leaning on the doorframe, his arms folded with his scowl fixed on her. Even with his displeasure, Polly felt her pulse skip a little. Right from the beginning, she had thought Morgan was magnificent. Brooding, but magnificent. Months after meeting him, while Morgan may have softened towards her, Polly still felt on the back foot with the man. There was something about the handsome marshal that pulled her to him. At times, she could swear he felt the same, even if Morgan denied it. The anger in his eyes was all too evident but even so, her mouth went dry and her belly fluttered. She swallowed and fixed him with a cool stare.

"I am. You got a problem with that?"

"You're not a lawman, Polly. I am," Morgan growled. "Let me do my job."

"You think a woman can't track a man?"

Polly knew Morgan had agreed to this before. His bride-to-be, Sheila, had been at his side and knew how to hunt a criminal as well as he did. Until she had been shot and killed in front of him, dying in his arms. Morgan had almost broken down telling her about this a few months back. It was over a decade ago since it happened, but it had made him cut himself off from everyone. None of his family knew about the impending wedding. He had planned to surprise them when they came back to town. Polly knew how much it still hurt him, and Morgan wanted it to stay that way.

Polly had never broken his trust. She understood his concerns, but she wasn't about to step back and do as he wished. Not this time. He had to know that.

"You'll just get in the way, Polly." Morgan pushed himself off the doorframe and stepped into the room. "You should stay here. You'll be a great help with Amy."

"Not a chance. I'm going to find that man and I'm going to make sure he pays."

Morgan tilted his head to the side and regarded her thoughtfully. Polly resisted the urge to squirm. Why did he have to use that look he put on criminals he was interrogating onto her? It was unnerving.

"You believe you'll be able to bring him in on your own?" Morgan asked.

Polly folded her arms.

"You underestimate me, Morgan. You know that my father was a tracker and a sniper in the war. He taught me how to follow someone and how to do it well. I can do your job as well as you can."

"You're still not coming with me."

Polly snorted. "I wasn't asking for your permission. I'm going out there, whether you like it or not."

"Polly..." Morgan groaned, but Polly swiped her hand through the air.

"No, don't start that with me! You think I'm going to sit here twiddling my thumbs while my friend's father gets away? That's not my style. I'm going to get after him and I'll make sure he pays for what he's done."

"And if Growcott hurts you as well?" Morgan shot back. "He might even succeed in killing you if it came to it."

Polly lifted her chin. "As I said, my father was a soldier. I can look after myself."

Morgan knew this. He had applauded her for

standing up for herself, even if it did frustrate him. So why was he against this now? He knew Polly would put up a fight. She was fiercely loyal and loved her friends dearly. She would do anything for them. Morgan had to know getting in the way was pointless.

"I won't let you go anywhere, Polly," Morgan said quietly, his eyes drifting over her face. "You need to stay here."

"Why?" Polly snapped. "Just tell me why I need to stay. Because you haven't given me a good enough reason." She scowled. "Is it because you're scared I'll end up like Sheila?" As soon as the words left her mouth, she wanted to snatch them back. Where did they even come from? How she hated her temper sometimes.

Morgan's expression didn't change, but his eyes darkened. Polly almost flinched as he stepped towards her, almost close enough to touch her. But even as his hand came up near her face, he didn't touch her. Now his hand closed into a fist, his jaw tightened as the first flicker of emotion passed across his face.

She shouldn't have pushed him that much, but Polly was past the point of caring. She was not going to be made to stay behind.

"Don't you ever mention her name again," Morgan hissed. "You don't have the right to do that."

"I think I've got my answer." Polly folded her arms. "If that isn't the answer, tell me why. It had better be a good reason because I won't take anything less."

Morgan was breathing heavily. Polly was surprised he hadn't reached out and grabbed her. He certainly looked like he wanted to shake her. Her heart was racing, but Polly was not about to back down. Not now. Morgan's nostrils flared and he growled.

"You have no idea how infuriating you are," he muttered.

"I've been told that often enough." Polly tossed her red hair over her shoulder. "The real Polly Brown doesn't sit back and let other people do the work. My friend was attacked and your brother was almost killed. I like your brother. I had to witness all that, and now you're telling me I have to let you take charge? It's not going to happen. I made a promise and I will keep it."

They glared at each other. Polly felt her breath lodge in her throat. She wished Morgan wouldn't stand this close; it was like she was unable to breathe properly. Just having Morgan in the room had her heart stuttering, but when he was close, it made all sense leave her. She had to focus on keeping calm. Morgan was just as infuriating and fiery when he wanted to be, and Polly liked a bit of fire. But theirs burned so brightly that it was a little frightening.

Finally, Morgan took a slow step back. He took a deep breath and let it out slowly.

"I'll be heading off shortly. If I find you out in the wilderness while I'm working, I'll make you go back. The more we argue, the more chance Growcott has of getting away. I'll probably never catch him if I'm dealing with you."

"Don't put it on me!" Polly shot back. "If you're that concerned, we can do it together. I won't be a hindrance."

Morgan was already shaking his head. "Absolutely not. I don't work with anyone."

"Why not?" Polly challenged. "You scared?"

Morgan was silent for a little too long. Polly tried not to shuffle from foot to foot. Then Morgan turned and strode towards the door.

"Do me a favor, Polly, and stay here. You'll be more useful here with Amy than out there with me."

Then he was gone before Polly could protest, slamming the door behind him.

CHAPTER THREE

Morgan set off at first light, packing some food and water that Amy had left out for him before riding out into the wilderness that surrounded Jefferson City. Being wounded, Growcott would need to stop and try to fix the injury or find someone who would. But the closest doctor was Morgan's own brother, and Morgan was sure Ernest would refuse to help someone who had just stabbed his brother. Ernest was still shaking in anger over it.

Morgan had to choose his path carefully. Growcott was not a local, so he would have no idea where he was going and so his path could be incredibly wild. Especially with the huge pack of wolves to the north of town. Morgan had no idea how many were in the pack, but there were enough to make him uncomfortable when he went that way. He could only hope that Growcott came across the wolves and they tore him to shreds. They liked a bit of blood.

This would have to be treated carefully. Tracking Dominic Growcott was one thing, but doing it without attracting the attention of the wild animals was going to be difficult. Morgan didn't really want a wolf or the odd mountain lion burying its teeth into him as he was trying to arrest someone.

That was another reason why Polly shouldn't come along. Morgan didn't want to think about her becoming wolf meat and that pack had been trouble recently.

As soon as she came to his mind he couldn't stop thinking about the annoying woman. Why did she have to be so frustrating? When he had met Polly for the first time, Morgan had told himself to keep away from her. Something told him she would be a challenge, and she was, but Morgan couldn't bring himself to stay back. She was enticing. Such beautiful red hair with a fiery temper to match. Morgan had never encountered anything like it. She was not afraid to stand up for her opinions and she was fiercely loyal to her sister, Tracy, as well as Amy. Not to mention that she was a very good baker, and Morgan found himself coming up to James' ranch more than he used to so he could sneak away with her baked goods or just simply talk to her.

They clearly got off on the wrong foot, and eventually, the two of them went from animosity to a grudging respect and then a friendship where they could talk and argue without getting too angry about the other's opinions. Morgan liked the unpredictable conversations; with his life, unpredictable was part of the package. He liked to be kept on his toes.

But Polly always had a way to knock him off-balance, and Morgan took forever to get back on even footing. He had to admit, she was one of a kind.

Much like Sheila. Sheila had been fierce and combative and very good at her job. Her parents had gotten furious when they found out their eighteen-year-old daughter wanted to go hunting fugitives with a twenty-three-year-old man, and they had disowned her. But Sheila hadn't cared. Neither had Morgan; he got the woman he had fallen in love with by his side.

Until she was killed and Morgan had been lost. Before that were the best days of his life. She spent nearly a year with him, while he courted her and grew to love her, their wedding was coming up, and then it was all gone. Morgan had never been so cold or lost before, but over time it faded a little. Now, fourteen years on, he occasionally felt a chill but he rarely thought about Sheila in the same way. When he did, it was with fondness, but she wouldn't have wanted him to mourn her forever. She would want him to move on.

The problem was, Morgan didn't think he could move on. Sheila had been it for him.

Then he met Polly. She was much like Sheila, but again, she wasn't Sheila. Only with her, Morgan had started thinking about what life would be like if he let Polly in. And every time he thought about it, he shut it out of his mind. Partly because it felt like a betrayal, but partly because he was a stubborn fool. He just kept telling himself it wasn't going to happen. Polly had been chosen, to an extent, by his father, and that meant if he gave in and married her, then Arnold Foster got a marriage he wanted and he won.

Morgan didn't want to give his father the satisfaction, even if it killed him to keep away from Polly.

He rode for an hour, heading up the slopes. When he got to the top he turned and looked back, Jefferson City spread out across the valley below. It was certainly a magnificent sight. Morgan took off his hat and with an old bandana, he wiped his brow. He hadn't anticipated that it would be this hot, and already he was feeling thirsty.

Dismounting, Morgan tied his horse to a nearby dead tree and got out his water skin. As he looked out over the sight before him, he found himself relieved that Polly was back at the ranch. This was not the place for her. Being on the ranch and keeping an eye on Amy was her job right now, not out here hunting for the man who tried to kidnap her friend. Polly was angry and she needed justice to be served, that Morgan could understand, but that didn't mean she could ride all across the range getting herself into trouble. Morgan had been born and raised in Jefferson City, so he knew the area. Polly would have been thrown in at the deep end. She would have ended up needing help, of that he was sure.

Of course, Morgan didn't think she was helpless, but

the wilderness of Missouri wasn't exactly a place that was easy for someone who wasn't a local. There was danger out here and he wanted Polly nowhere near it.

Yet even with all this, for a brief moment, he wished she was here. The view from the top of the hill, looking down on Jefferson City and its surrounding land, was magnificent. Polly would certainly appreciate it, and Morgan wanted to see the look on her face when she saw the sight before her.

There was a movement behind him, Morgan froze. Instinctively, his hand went to his pistol. Was it Growcott trying to sneak up on him? Or was it a wild animal? Either way, Morgan was not taking any chances.

With his pistol in his hand, Morgan turned. But he wasn't pointing the barrel at Growcott or a wolf sneaking upon him. Instead, he was taking aim at Polly as she trotted up along the slope, coming to a stop beside his horse. The animal gave her a bemused look as she slowed her mount to a stop and dismounted.

"I was beginning to think I would never catch you," she said.

"Polly?" Morgan lowered his gun. "What are you doing here?"

"I told you, I'm going after Growcott." Polly brushed down her shirt. "Whether you like it or not, I'm going. You can't push me into doing what you think I should be doing. You're just going to have to accept that I'm not backing down."

She had to be mad. For a moment, Morgan couldn't speak and he wasn't sure if it was anger, fear, or something entirely different. She was going to get herself killed. Never mind that she was armed and dressed for the hunt in riding boots, pants that fitted her legs nicely with a white blouse and jacket. A Stetson was perched neatly on her head with her hair plaited up over one shoulder. Even though she looked the part, completely at home, she was in the wrong place. Morgan knew that having her along was going to get him distracted.

Her eyes widened!

Morgan realized that he was openly staring at her and he shook himself. "No, you've got to go back. It's too dangerous for you out here," he blurted out and knew he sounded like a spoiled child.

"No more than it is for you." Polly shot back.

"That's not the point."

"I think it is." Polly lifted her chin and fixed him with a defiant glare. "I'm better at paying attention to the small things, more so than you. You've told me that yourself."

"Not in this situation." Morgan felt like tearing his hair out. Was the good Lord testing him? For he was sure he had never met a woman so stubborn since Sheila. "You need to go home, Polly."

He headed towards her, intending to guide her to her horse. He would escort her back, even if it meant losing Growcott's trail. That could be picked up again. Only Polly pulled away and pushed him hard in the chest.

"Don't you even think about it, Morgan Foster! You can force me back to the ranch if you want to, but I'll just keep coming back out. You'll spend more time dealing with me than you would looking for

Growcott. Do you want to waste time or do your job?"

Morgan growled. He really wanted to shake her. "I'm doing my job by keeping you safe," he snapped.

"I can handle myself." Polly folded her arms, cocking her hip. "You don't need to worry about me, Morgan. You just need to watch your own back... and maybe I can help with that... maybe we could be a team?"

Morgan could watch his own back. He had been doing it for over a decade and he had largely been successful. Now was not the time to tell Polly of the times he had almost been run through by people he had been searching for; that would just give her more reason to stay.

But he couldn't force her back. Morgan knew that he should, but he couldn't. And from the way her eyes were gleaming, she knew it. Morgan took a deep breath and slowly counted to ten before he responded.

"Did your father tell you that you're an incredibly stubborn woman?"

Polly smirked. "Who do you think I inherited the stubbornness from? Look, I'm not here to discuss this. I know what I'm going to do. You can come along with me or do it on your own. It's up to you. But you're not going to send me back. That's not going to happen."

They glared at each other. Morgan was the first to break the stare, looking away as he took his Stetson off, running his hand through his hair with a heavy sigh.

"All right, fine. You can come along. But you need to do as I say. This is my livelihood, and I know what I'm doing. You are not a lawman... woman," he backtracked quickly as Polly arched an eyebrow, "so you do as I say and don't do anything rash if you come across Growcott first. You're a civilian. If you kill him, I'll have to arrest you instead."

Was there a flicker in her expression? Had she been intending to do just that? Then the flicker was gone and Polly nodded her head.

"Don't worry. I won't do anything stupid. I promise."

"I don't believe that."

She smiled and it almost dropped him to his knees. "I

know. But at least you know where we stand now." Polly turned and went to her horse. "Are we going now? Growcott's injured, but he can still cover a lot of ground."

Morgan could only stare as Polly mounted her horse and adjusted herself in the saddle. He had never seen her ride a horse and hadn't realized a woman could look so graceful just sitting in the saddle. He shook himself. He had to stop getting distracted, or he was going to end up making a mistake. In front of Polly, that was going to be embarrassing... in his line of work it could be worse than that, it could be a death sentence for either of them.

Sighing, he tied his water skin to his saddle and untied his horse from the tree.

"Fine. Let's go, then."

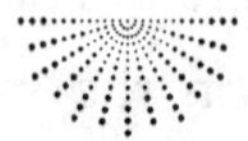

CHAPTER FOUR

Polly glanced at Morgan as they made their way down the slope and into the trees. They had seen some signs a little way back that suggested that Growcott had come this way. Now they were heading towards the river; there they would water the horses and check to see if they could find more tracks. Any person, no matter how mad they were, would always look for a water source. Both for drinking and for following to the next town. That would be a long way, but at least the man wouldn't be going around in circles.

They had been going on for nearly two hours now, and there wasn't much to indicate that Growcott was still on this trail. Polly's mouth was dry and she was hungry and hot, but she wasn't going to complain about this to Morgan. She didn't want to give him any reason to think she couldn't handle this. Polly was going to find Dominic Growcott and she wasn't going to back down.

When Amy had first come to stay with them after running away from home, Polly made a promise to her friend that she would always protect her. She had almost failed when Growcott found them, and she wasn't about to slip up again.

Tracy would call her mad. She had called her mad, reminding her that she shouldn't behave in such a manner, but Polly didn't care. When she gave her word, she kept it. Tracy might find it ridiculous to go to such lengths, as might Amy, but this was how Polly had grown up. Her father had been like that when he was alive, and she had inherited his mannerisms and single-mindedness. She admitted that it was a flaw of hers, but there was no way she could change.

Morgan was going to have to get used to it.

She scanned the ground around them as they headed through the trees. It was cooler under the spread of branches; with less sun getting through it gave her a little relief. Who knew that it would be so warm at Christmas-time? Polly had only ever encountered snow at this time of year, so this heat was a novelty. In many ways, she had always hated the snow. It was pretty but far too cold. She preferred the warmer climate.

Then she saw it. On a tree trunk. It was a smudge just out of sight and could be dismissed at a glance, but it was there. Polly pulled her horse to a stop and dismounted.

"Polly?" Morgan slowed his horse and turned in his saddle. "Where are you going?"

"One moment."

Polly inspected the tree, inspecting the smudge. It could have been tree sap, but this was a different color. Possibly red. It looked like blood.

There was more blood on a nearby stone, and it was still fresh. Polly's fingers came away red.

"It's blood." She turned to Morgan. "Growcott came this way, and not too long ago."

Morgan frowned. "How do you know this isn't animal blood?"

Polly smiled and pointed.

"Because I can see the print of a boot over there. I don't think many animals have started wearing human clothing."

Morgan looked, leaning over in the saddle. Sure enough, there was a footprint in the dirt. Polly could clearly make it out now. It was certainly the shape of an adult boot and not the paw of a wild animal. Morgan frowned.

"I would have missed that," he muttered with a shake of his head.

"I know." Polly grinned.

"You did well spotting these, I'll give you that, but that doesn't mean you're better at tracking."

"You didn't spot the blood, did you?" Polly got back into the saddle and smirked at him. "Once you get sharp eyes, you'll be able to see for yourself."

Morgan arched an eyebrow. Then he looked away and groaned. "You are so infuriating."

"You've already told me that." Polly tilted her head to the side and listened. "I can hear water. Are we close to the river now?"

"It's just up ahead." Morgan urged his horse into motion. "This way."

They broke through the trees and into a clearing, the slope flattening out towards the river and a multitude of rocks were scattered around the bank. Polly was stunned just looking at this. She hadn't been too impressed with Jefferson City when she first arrived, but she had come to appreciate her surroundings, and this... it was just beautiful.

Morgan held up a hand and signaled for her to stop. Then he climbed off his horse, tying the reins to a nearby tree. Polly did the same, keeping her hand on her rifle slung across her back. She had hoped she wouldn't need to use it, even if there was a great temptation to push the barrel of the rifle into Growcott's face and pull the trigger.

Sometimes in her anger, she wanted to do that but it wasn't here. Maybe she wasn't brave enough to do that, but the thought was always there.

Polly followed Morgan onto the rocks and climbed down to what looked to be a little cave, open to the water but out of sight of people passing by. It looked like the perfect place to hide out, quiet, and away from prying eyes of both the human and animal variety. From the look of it, someone else had had the same idea.

There were the remains of a shirt lying in tatters on the ground. One sleeve had been ripped off, while the other was covered in blood.

"Growcott's been here recently." Morgan crouched and picked up the shirt, inspecting the sleeve. "The blood's drying, but it's still damp. It looks like he tried to make a bandage out of one of the sleeves."

"So, he's going shirtless in the wilderness." Polly looked around. "He's badly wounded, so he couldn't have gone far."

"James shot him in the wrist, not the leg, so he wouldn't be completely hindered."

"Unless he's suffering from blood loss. That makes people slow down."

"I won't argue with that," Morgan grunted. He

looked up and frowned. "Are you all right? You're looking very pale."

"I'm fine." Polly managed a smile. "Why shouldn't I be?"

"Well, you are swaying right now." Morgan rose to his feet. "Are you sure you're all right? You look like you're about to collapse."

Polly thought about lying but then decided against it. She couldn't lie to him, and Morgan wouldn't be impressed if she tried. She leaned against a rock as the world tilted again.

"I just missed breakfast, that's all. I couldn't eat it." Polly grimaced and pressed a hand to her stomach as it growled. "I wanted to get after you, and I was too edgy to eat."

"Well, you're a fool." Morgan shook his head and took her arm. "Come with me."

Polly thought about arguing, but her hunger was catching up to her. The heat of the sun wasn't helping much, either. She could feel a headache coming on, and it felt like it was squeezing her head. Morgan helped her back to their horses and then made her sit on a flat rock before rifling through his bag. Polly sat up straight, slipping her rifle off her back and laying it next to her.

"I'm fine, really."

Morgan snorted.

"You need to eat, Polly. You should've made yourself eat something before you came to find me." He brought out something wrapped in a cloth and brought it over. "You're no good to anyone if you don't take care of yourself properly. Now, eat."

He held it out, and Polly saw that it was one of the bread rolls she had made the day before. She took it and managed to take a bite. She was hungry, but her stomach still felt like it was about to churn and bring anything back up. However, Morgan was right. She was going to end up collapsing and be of no use to anyone if she didn't eat and drink.

Polly managed to eat the roll, washing it down with water from her skin that Morgan handed her. He watered the horses and then sat cross-legged on the ground in front of her, watching her intently. It was as if he was going to force the food down her throat if she didn't eat. Was that a flash of concern in his eyes? Polly was too worn out to think much right now.

It didn't take long to finish eating, and it was only then that Morgan spoke.

"Better?"

"Much better, thank you."

They sat together in silence for a little while longer. Polly could feel the atmosphere change between them. It had been tense for the last few hours since she had caught up to Morgan, both of them choosing only to speak when really needing to. But now it was... comfortable. There was still a bit of tension, but it felt better. Much like it had been once they got past the initial discomfort of their first meetings. Polly had enjoyed those times when Morgan came back to the ranch saying he was coming to talk to James, only for him to sit in the kitchen for several hours while she worked or baked.

It was a strange thing for her to come to be comfortable with such a brooding, mysterious man like Morgan Foster. He had chosen to keep himself aloof from everyone else, even his brothers and the six of them were very close. But as time went on, the two of them began talking more about their lives. Polly had spoken about her father, whom she had loved dearly, and her mother for the first time since her parents died, and Morgan ended up opening up about the time he was secretly engaged. Polly was shocked that not even his brothers knew about Sheila. Looking back on it, she understood why Morgan was reluctant to get married. It was both because no one could replace Sheila and also because he was scared of losing someone again.

But she wasn't Sheila. And Polly wished that Morgan could realize now that just because he was in a dangerous position didn't mean he couldn't have some happiness. Polly could only hope that he saw her as someone who could be considered a good choice.

Because if I keep going on like this, I'm going to end up having my heart broken.

That was another reason why she had come along with him. Polly just wanted to be with him.

She looked down at the water skin still in her hands.

"I'm sorry, Morgan."

"What for?"

Polly took a deep breath. For all of her confidence, she couldn't bring herself to look at him.

"For bringing Sheila into this last night. You're right, I spoke out of turn. And I shouldn't have said anything about her. That's not fair on you. I..." Polly shrugged. "My temper tends to get in the way."

Morgan didn't say anything. Polly risked a glance up, only to find him watching her with a slight smile. Even with a slight relaxation of his expression, his eyes would sparkle. Oh, he really was handsome, and he didn't seem to realize it. Polly's heart stuttered a few beats and her mouth went dry.

Then Morgan reached out and took the water skin from her fingers, tightening the stopper and put it to one side.

"You're right. You shouldn't have brought her up. But I forgive you."

"You do?"

"Yes." Morgan gave a lopsided shrug. "I've been known to let my temper get in the way. Mostly when I was younger."

"You're still like that now." Polly giggled.

"Ouch."

"It's true." Polly sat forward. "You like to think you're in more control because you're the oldest brother and you're not as hot-headed as before. You're still that, but it's changed. It's a little more... brooding."

"Brooding?" Morgan arched an eyebrow. "You think I'm broody?"

"I couldn't think of the exact word." Polly bit her lip. "It's a little darker than that. It's like you're trying to hide that lighter side of you. A side I've seen briefly in the past."

Morgan regarded her for a moment. Then he rubbed his hands over his face.

"It's easier to remain separated by keeping people away. It doesn't seem to have worked on you, though."

"Not really. I'm more curious."

"I've noticed that." Morgan's expression warmed as he looked at her. "You're not like any other woman, Polly Brown. You're far more interesting than that."

Polly didn't know what to say to that. She had been given compliments before, but some of them were rather offhanded or backhanded comments. The only compliments she had gotten outside of her family were from Amy and her new friends who had come with her to Jefferson City. James had become another one as well. And now Morgan.

Although, Morgan had been praising her from the beginning. They had started as backhanded comments, but soon they turned into genuine praise. Polly could remember each and every compliment and they always made her warm inside.

"Can I ask you something, Polly?"

Polly blinked. Morgan was still staring at her. She cleared her throat and shifted on the rock. "It will depend on what you want to ask."

"Why did you come to Jefferson City? What did you think you were coming out here to get?"

Polly frowned. Now that was an odd question at this time. "Didn't you ask me before?"

"No, I didn't. And I was too wrapped up in my own anger to really ask what you wanted." Morgan leaned his elbows on his knees as he watched her. "Did you come out here for a marriage or for something else?"

Polly hesitated. She could tell him it was for marriage, but that would be a lie. In the beginning, it would be. Now, she wasn't so sure. Even if she confessed that Morgan might guess what she really wanted now. She took a deep breath and chose her words carefully.

"I don't know, really. After our parents died, Tracy and I were alone. Our extended families were far away, and none of them were willing to take us in. We weren't what they were expecting of young ladies. We didn't fit the mold and they refused to have anything to do with us."

"Fit what mold?"

"I have no idea, but that's what my aunt said when she was speaking for my grandmother. I'm still trying to figure it out." Polly tugged on her braid. "They started harassing us to marry. Saying that marriage was the only thing we could do with ourselves now. Several of our neighbors started in on it as well as if it was their business. Tracy and I got so many offers we were going mad. Neither of us wanted to marry those who offered it as they tended to be people we disliked."

Morgan arched an eyebrow. "Surely, there were some decent men around?"

"Not for a while. Mother had turned herself into something of a matchmaker, and she was quite good at it. Unfortunately, that meant all the decent men were not available, and those who were got put off by the fact I liked to shoot and speak my mind while Tracy's quick wit and silent defiance was not considered desirable." Polly still hadn't got her head around that. "Everyone made it sound like we had no option except to get married. I mean, who heard of two unmarried sisters living in a house our father owned and not having a man in charge?"

"It's happened before. We've got a few people in that situation here."

"Not where we lived." Polly made a face. "Our small town was backward."

Morgan's mouth twitched.

"I can imagine. Women are in short supply out

here... that came out wrong but you know what I mean. Even so, if a woman was to want to live alone no one would mind. She might get offers. But even then, nobody's pressured."

"I wish I'd grown up here," Polly muttered. "Then Tracy and I wouldn't have had any problems once our parents died."

Maybe I might have met Morgan before now.

Stop it. Not now.

"Is that why you and your sister replied to Pastor Tom's advert for unmarried women?" Morgan asked. "Just to get away from all of that?"

"Pretty much. Amy, too." Polly shrugged. "We thought we would get a better chance here than back home. Even if we didn't end up with a marriage, we could start afresh. No one to tell us what to do as they had at home. No one to tell me that I'm not ladylike and I'm never going to find a husband." She giggled. "I think most of the men were put off by the fact that I could shoot a target better than they could."

"You really did that?"

"I did. And then I'd be called all sorts of names for knowing how to use a rifle so well." Polly sighed. "I couldn't win."

"Hmm." Morgan tilted his head to one side. "Those men didn't know what they were missing."

Polly stared. "What? You think I'm ladylike?"

"I didn't say that. But they clearly don't see what I see."

Polly's mouth went dry. She licked her lips and saw Morgan's eyes drop to her mouth. *Did his eyes just flash?* Polly gulped.

"What do you see when you look at me, then?" she asked in a hoarse whisper.

For a moment, she thought Morgan was going to respond to her, but then he looked away and rose to his feet while clearing his throat.

"The horses are rested, we'd better get going again. Growcott can't be too far away now."

Polly stared at him. What had just happened there? She rose to her feet, swaying a little. She had been so close to getting through to Morgan, and now he was pulling away again. Just like every other time. Even when their conversations opened each other up more than talking to anyone else, Morgan still closed up when it got too... personal? Polly didn't know what to say about it.

Morgan had picked up the water skin and was fastening it to his horse's saddle, his back to her. Polly debated with herself for a moment. She was known for being impulsive and when she did something, she went headfirst into it. But when it came to Morgan, she couldn't do it. Her nerves seemed to get the better of her.

But not this time. She was going to take a step forward.

"Morgan?"

Morgan turned, his expression now blank. Polly squared her shoulders and approached him. Morgan was much taller than her, but she managed to tug him down by his shirt. He started as she kissed him, but then he groaned and wrapped his arms around her and tugged her against him. Polly let go of his shirt and her arms went around his neck, allowing Morgan to take charge of the kiss.

She had expected fire, but nothing like this. Morgan's kiss burned hotly, warming her all over. He cradled her against his chest, cupping her head like she was the most delicate creature even as he deepened the kiss. Polly could feel herself trembling. Or was it Morgan? She didn't know and, quite frankly, she didn't care.

Morgan broke the kiss, slowly pulling back and leaving feather-light kisses on her mouth. Then he stared at her, still holding her in his embrace.

"What was that for?"

"I..." Polly swallowed. Her heart felt like it was about to burst out of her chest. "I just wanted to say thank you."

"For what? I haven't done anything yet."

"You have." Polly lowered her arms and stepped back. Morgan let her go. "Much more than you realize."

Now that tension was back, and it was awkward. Morgan stared at her in bewilderment. Then he turned away, adjusting his Stetson before getting up into the saddle.

"Come on, let's go," he said gruffly. "We're not going to get this man if we stand here talking."

There he was. Shutting himself off again. Polly swallowed and went to her horse, picking up her rifle as an afterthought. Morgan hadn't waited for her to mount; he was already heading along the river.

CHAPTER FIVE

Tension hung in the air between them. Polly stared at Morgan's back as he headed along the bank, following the river downstream. She wanted to say something, but what could you say after practically throwing yourself on a man and him then walking away?

Polly didn't regret the kiss. She was glad she had done it, especially now that she knew Morgan was just as affected by the kiss as she was. But now her nerves were starting to take over. Had she done wrong? Had she ruined whatever they had between them? How she hoped she hadn't. Morgan may have responded strongly to the kiss, but now he had withdrawn so much she was beginning to worry.

They were going to be having a very long talk later, she just knew it. Right now, they had a job to do, someone to look for. Thinking about an impending conversation was not going to help. It certainly didn't help that Polly couldn't stop thinking about the touch of his lips. She touched her own lips, remembering the moment Morgan cradled her in his arms. A smile spread across her face.

It was certainly worth it.

Soon, the trees ended and the river widened and ran down into a waterfall, spreading out into a lagoon below. It was surrounded by emerald green grass with white rocks that seemed to glow like gems under the sun. Polly stared in amazement.

"Whoa. This is beautiful."

"I love this place and always think of it as a little slice of heaven." Morgan glanced over his shoulder. It was the first time he had looked at her since their kiss. "But it's barely used. It's a popular place for wild animals, especially wolves and mountain lions. It's not a good idea to be out here alone when there are so many predators looking for their next meal."

Polly shuddered. "I think I've gone off the place now."

"I don't blame you." Morgan shook his head. "I remember my brothers and I coming here a few times when we were young, thinking we would be fine. We didn't get on with Father back then, either. It was only when Ernest got bitten by a mountain lion that tried to drag him away, that we realized that his fears weren't unfounded."

Polly stared at him. "Ernest was almost killed by a mountain lion?"

"It ripped into his arm." Morgan tapped his arm. "You must have seen the scars."

"I have, and he told me the story, but I thought it was him trying to flirt with me."

Morgan laughed. That simple sound had Polly resisting the urge to shiver as warmth tickled down her spine.

"My brother's attentions have been firmly on Jacira since she came into town, even if he won't openly admit it. When he says something, he certainly means it."

"Well, now I feel a fool for telling him off for selling such a tale." Polly looked at a gathering of rocks across the lagoon. "What's over there? It looks like a series of caves."

"That's right. It's where a wolf pack was taking shelter during the night or when it's very hot. Another reason why this isn't a place to play."

"Do you think Growcott might be in there?"

Morgan frowned. "It's possible, but he would be playing with his own life if the pack is still using it. At this time, they might be hunting."

"That's a point. Even so..." Polly moved her horse to go around Morgan's and pull up beside him. "Shall we go down, then?"

Morgan shook his head. "It's best that we don't, Polly. I don't want you getting hurt."

"I'll be fine." Polly patted her rifle. "I can shoot."

"And that will scare anything that is trapped. There is nothing more dangerous than a trapped wolf. It's best that we stay out of there." Morgan pointed down the hill before them. "We can go down here and circle around. If Growcott's come this way on foot, he would have gone this way."

Polly frowned. "So, we're not going in to look? It's a perfect place to go and hide if you were on the run."

Morgan scowled. "What did I just say? Even I'm not brave enough to go into a literal wolf's den."

Polly sighed and nudged her horse into motion. "But I'm not you, am I?"

"Polly... Polly!"

Polly could hear Morgan shouting after her as she trotted down the slope. As it got steeper, she jumped off and led her horse towards the caves. She was armed and she had plenty of ammunition. There was no fear. She had seen wolves and a mountain lion before, if you shot at them, they would run away instead of charging.

Polly could only hope that she was right and that she wasn't being a complete fool with her life.

Her horse started getting skittish as they got closer, stopping abruptly and refusing to get any closer. Polly stroked her beast's neck and looped the reins over a rock. The horse was still skittish, what could it smell?

"All right, girl, you stay here. I'll be fine."

Even as she said that she could feel her heart racing. Facing down a pack of wolves wasn't what she was keen on doing, but her desire to chase Dominic Growcott and capture him took over her common sense. She was adamant that this was going to happen. She had made a promise and she was following through.

Polly could only silently pray that Morgan wouldn't need to rescue her.

Chambering a round in her rifle, Polly approached the caves. Even from where she was, they looked like a complete maze. It would take a while to search each of them to see if anyone - or anything - was there. And with Morgan refusing to come down, she would have to do it herself.

I'll show him that I'm capable. I can do this.

Maybe this is one time where my impulsive behavior is going to get me into trouble.

Polly paused as she reached the first cave. She

listened, but all she could hear was the waterfall. It was too loud to hear anything else. This was going to be interesting. Gripping her rifle tightly, she eased around a rock and checked the first cave. It was merely a hole in the rock, a shallow shelter from the sun.

Maybe she should go back. Morgan was right; this could be dangerous, it could be more than she could handle.

Polly's heart was racing, her breath coming in short blasts but she had to do this. She had made a promise and if she didn't stop him, she wondered if her friend would ever be safe. She had a rifle. That would be enough, wouldn't it?

The first cave was empty and just a shallow dugout. The path was well worn but too hard to make out footprints or animal tracks so she eased herself further along and the sun was cut off by the rocks above. The cold made this all the more real and she shivered.

Keeping going, she peered around at the next cave. There were a series of passages of rock and dark entrances opening up in places. Swallowing, she swung her rifle around and followed where it went. Her finger poised over the trigger.

It was a bit of a tight squeeze through some of the passages. The further she went in, the more Polly decided that Growcott couldn't have come this way; he was a much bigger man and he would have got himself stuck in the gaps.

The other caves seemed to be empty. Polly wasn't going to venture too far into the darkness, not without a light source. If there was a mountain lion or wolves further in them, she wouldn't know. Same if a man was bleeding out in there. Polly was beginning to hope that Growcott did die of his wounds before they found him, then they wouldn't have to deal with him.

Shaking her head, she whispered a quick prayer. That was unchristian, he should be brought to justice. Only that was easier said than done. She doubted he would come easy and her need to keep Amy safe called for blood. Polly wasn't normally unkind, but with Dominic Growcott she lost all motivation to be nice. He lost that when he tried to force his daughter into a life of pain and misery.

Polly had checked most of the caves when she heard a growl. She froze, turning slowly towards the sound. Then she saw it. A huge grey wolf was near the river. It hadn't spotted her and was lying in the sun and stretching out. Polly's heart was in her mouth and she shrank back against the cave wall, freezing. Why hadn't she listened? For a moment her instinct was to panic and run, but she couldn't take her eyes off the sight. It was truly remarkable.

Taking a slow silent breath, she took stock of the situation. A slight breeze on her face told her the wind was towards her. That was good, her scent would not alert the beast. There was plenty of cover, she had only just moved to a spot where the wolf could see her and she could see it. If she backed out the same way she would, probably, be able to make her way back unseen. If she was careful and lucky!

Softer sounds caught her attention. Sounds of yapping and high-pitched snarling drew her eyes from the wolf and down to the river bank. There was movement at the edge of the water, just out of sight. Carefully, Polly shifted around the rocks and moved into a crouch, her rifle at the ready. She didn't want to shoot unless she had to, but it didn't hurt to be ready.

Her heart melted when she saw the cubs. There were three of them playing along the edge of the water, jumping on each other in a rough-and-tumble game. Polly watched as one ran around the others and over to the adult. She had to be the mother, she barely reacted as one of her cubs started jumping on her, playing with her tail as it flapped lazily around its head.

It was just an adorable sight that Polly was transfixed for a moment. But was not prepared to move, as she understood the danger she was in. The situation was even worse than she thought as the mother would fight to protect her cubs. She didn't know if wolf cubs could tear limbs off like the adults, but she didn't want to wait around to find out.

It's a pity Morgan isn't here to see this. He would find this just as beautiful as I do.

The mother sniffed the air, rose to her feet, and growled. The cubs clambered out of the water and lumbered over to her, still jumping at each other and patting their siblings away with large paws. The mother picked one cub up by the scruff of its neck and started to carry it away along the narrow path at the edge of the river. The other two followed, still tumbling over each other with excited yips.

It was only when they moved out of sight that Polly could breathe properly again. She lowered the rifle, realizing that her hands were shaking. That was the most beautiful but most terrifying thing she had ever witnessed. While Polly was glad to have captured such a moment, she was even more relieved to have come out of it alive.

Perhaps she had better get back to Morgan. He would be worried sick about her; in fact, she was surprised he hadn't come after her. A smile came over her face as her heartbeat slowed to normal. She had something to tell him.

Easing off the wall she turned to walk back and then gasped as someone grabbed her braid and yanked her backward. The rifle fell from her hands and clattered on the rocks. Polly tried to swing her arms back, flailing as she was almost lifted off her feet. Then she froze when something cold and sharp pressed against her neck.

"You fight, and I'll slit your throat."

Growcott. He really was here. Polly swallowed,

flinching as the blade of the knife rubbed against her skin. She tried not to panic, but her heart was racing so fast that she was becoming lightheaded.

"Growcott."

"You shouldn't have followed me out here, Miss Brown," Growcott growled. "You should've stayed away."

"You were a fool to come here for Amy."

Growcott shoved her hard. Polly stumbled and lost her footing, falling off the narrow ledge and onto the uneven ground below. Her hip exploded in pain, as did her elbow. She tried to sit up, but her legs refused to move at first. She silently prayed that nothing was broken.

A shadow loomed over her. Polly looked up to see Growcott standing above her. The man was a mess. He was pale, almost translucent, and wearing his jacket over a bare chest. The remains of his shirt were wrapped around his wrist, and it was soaked through with blood. He was holding the knife in his left hand.

Swaying slightly, the man looked like he was about to topple over.

Polly glanced at his wrist. "Hurts, does it?"

"Like hell. Bullet's still in there." Growcott's bared his teeth. "When I get back, that Foster brat is going to get what's coming to him."

"If you get near him. You'll be arrested as soon as you come back."

"For what?"

"Attempted murder, for a start." Polly sat up. Her elbow and hip were now throbbing, the pain making her eyes water. "Sheriff Foster is alive, thankfully."

Growcott grunted. "Pity. I would prefer that he was dead. All of those Foster brats should be dead."

"I'm sure others would argue that point." Polly glanced at her rifle. Could she get to it before Growcott did? "You should've left Amy alone. She left because she didn't want to be a pawn in your games of chance."

"She had duties at home to tend to. She needed to come back."

Polly snorted. "What duties? Being forced into a marriage with an old man just so you can get more money? You would just break that contract when all that money is gone and use her for something else. Amy didn't want that, no woman would. We were more than happy to help her getaway."

"It was family business, Miss Brown. Not your business."

"Try again." Polly lifted her chin, even as she resisted the urge to quiver. "Amy wanted out, and she's my friend. That makes it my business."

"And now she's with a man who works cattle? What could she possibly get from him? He's not rich."

"He's wealthy enough."

"He's not useful to me."

Polly almost burst out laughing.

"Not useful because he wouldn't help you out of the hole you put yourself in? James would have helped you if you had been a respectful person and treated Amy as you should treat a daughter. But you abused her and used her for your own gain. James won't stand for that. He loves her."

"Love?" Growcott rolled his eyes. "What is love?"

"You married Amy's mother, didn't you? That should mean something."

"She came from a wealthy family. We both knew it wasn't for love. That I needed to sort my debts out." Growcott's face darkened, bringing his pallor to a vague pale color. "And then that was cut off from me when they didn't appreciate that I needed help."

Polly stared. Amy had said her family had cut Growcott off but had never been given the reason why. She didn't think she would hear someone speak so callously about the woman they had been married to for years.

It was always about the money. Even back then as a young man. The money came first for Dominic Growcott. His wife and daughter were an afterthought. If they couldn't help him financially, he didn't care about them. Now Amy could bring some value to him, he was coming after her to get what he wanted, ignoring what Amy wanted. His own daughter meant nothing beyond lots of money.

"You're disgusting," Polly spat. "Amy did the right

thing leaving. And now you're going to pay for trying to kidnap her and attempting to murder the sheriff."

"You can't be tried for kidnapping if the 'captor' is the parent."

"You can, and Amy will press charges." Polly moved onto her knees, shifting slowly into a crouch. "When someone says no, you should listen to them."

If she pounced now, she could probably get to the rifle before Growcott grabbed at her. From the way he was starting to sway, Growcott wouldn't be able to move as fast. He had been bleeding too much. It was a wonder the wolves hadn't come after him.

"No one's arresting me." Growcott sniggered and held up the knife in his hand. "I'm getting out of here and then I'm coming back with reinforcements. Amy will be coming home."

"Even though she may be married by the time you come back?"

"A marriage is no marriage if I don't give permission."

Polly snorted. "She doesn't need permission. And you don't have permission to kidnap her."

She flinched as Growcott pointed the blade at her face, the tip loomed large in her eyes and looked mere inches away. Polly held her ground and didn't even flinch. Growcott thrived on being menacing. Polly wouldn't be bullied.

"I'm her father, Miss Brown. I can do what I want with her. And you can't tell me otherwise."

"Growcott!"

Polly almost collapsed with relief when she heard Morgan's voice. He was approaching them from the lagoon where the cubs had been frolicking, his gun pointed at Growcott's head. Polly's heart stopped racing when she saw him. Just seeing him was such a relief.

Whispering a quick prayer of thanks, she knew this nightmare would soon be over.

Growcott's eyes widened when he saw Morgan. Then with a snarl he drew back his arm and flung the knife in Morgan's direction. Polly screamed as Morgan ducked, the knife going way over his head. Then Growcott was gone, staggering over the rocks and out of sight.

Morgan rose to his feet and ran to Polly, falling to his knees beside her.

"Are you all right?"

"I'm fine." Polly pointed at Growcott. "Get after him."

"What about you?"

"I'll follow you. Go!"

Morgan hesitated, but then he scrambled up and ran after Growcott.

CHAPTER SEVEN

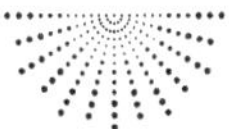

For a man who was suffering from blood loss, Growcott could certainly move fast. Morgan charged after him, scrambling over the rocks and coming out on the other side of the caves. The lagoon narrowed back into a river, only this part was a lot wider than upstream with the water faster-moving. The sound of the water was deafening, and Morgan could feel his head hurting as he ran along the bank.

Growcott was further downstream, stumbling over smaller rocks, an upturned tree with its roots sticking out, and bumped into another tree where its leaves overhung the river. It was there that he fell down, landing hard on the ground. Morgan heard his gasp even over the water.

He picked up his pace and ducked under the branches, standing over Growcott as the man tried to get up again.

"It's over, Growcott." Morgan pointed his pistol at Growcott's face. "Let's get you back to Jefferson City. You're going to bleed out if you don't get medical attention."

"Medical attention from your brother?" Growcott sneered. "That sounds like a death sentence."

"You already have a potential death sentence. Kidnapping, attempted murder, do you want the charges to stack up any further?"

Growcott didn't get up. He just lay there, clutching at his wrist. He was looking so white that Morgan was surprised that he hadn't passed out already.

Morgan glanced at Growcott's injured wrist. Blood was now soaking through the makeshift bandage and smearing over the man's fingers.

"Running away from the nearest medical help is not

going to make you any better. You're going to end up dying if you carry on this way."

"I'll live. I've dealt with worse," Growcott grunted. "When you've been beaten as much as I have, this is nothing."

"Well, this time you're truly beaten."

The two men glared at each other. Morgan could see Growcott wanted to fight, but he was rapidly losing his strength. It had been a day since he had been shot, and without a doctor, he could bleed out or even lose his hand. While Morgan would happily let either of those options happen, he knew that he couldn't do that to Amy. He was still her father, even after everything he had done.

"All she had to do was do as she was told and marry." Growcott's breathing was labored. "Then we wouldn't have had any problems. We would be safe."

"You wouldn't be safe, and you know it." Morgan saw the man shift on the ground and moved back out of reach. "Even in the back of your mind, you know it wouldn't stop. You would keep doing it again and again, and then there really would be nothing left.

Do you really want to put your daughter through all that?"

"I'm her family. She should've done as she was told!"

"You're her father, you should have cared for her, cherished her, and kept her safe."

Morgan couldn't believe he was having this conversation with a grown man. The last time he had had a conversation with a spoiled individual was when Chris was eight years old having a tantrum because he didn't get the Christmas gifts he wanted. Morgan had been the one to scold him, only to have his father warn him not to push it too far as it was his job to discipline Chris.

And then he had gone on to spoil Chris even more. It was a wonder that Chris had grown up to be a decent man. With the example they had it was a wonder that any of them had grown up well. Talking to Growcott was almost like talking to his father; the words were going in but they weren't resonating because it wasn't what they wanted to hear.

"Why can't you let her be happy, admit that you messed up with her? If you were to be a man about your mistakes, then we would help you. My family isn't above helping those who admit they need someone to get them through their mess. For Amy, we would maybe even let you go."

Growcott scoffed and looked away. "You wouldn't help me. You'd send me home to face ruin."

"You ruined yourself years ago. But if we had helped…"

"I don't need your help." Growcott struggled to sit up. It took him a few goes, and it was clearly a strain. "I can get out of this. If Amy comes back with me…"

"That's not going to happen."

Morgan was sure that Growcott was going to start fighting. Even though he was badly wounded and there was a gun pointed at him, he was still gearing up to fight. Morgan shook his head.

"I'd stay down, if I were you, Growcott. You're not going to win."

"Oh, I'm going to win." Growcott moved very slowly onto his knees. His breathing was even more labored. "You're not taking me back except to escort me to get

Amy. Then we're going home. And you're going to leave me alone."

"I can't do that. You committed a crime. You have to pay for it."

Growcott scoffed. "Not if you don't catch me."

"Are you serious? You can't even stand up right now."

"I'd like to see you try and run," Polly's voice was low and menacing.

Growcott blinked and looked around. Morgan also looked, and there he saw Polly appear through the trees. Her rifle was pointed at Growcott, her aim unwavering. Growcott bared his teeth, his voice barely a snarl.

"You think you're going to kill me, you little…"

"I'm not going to kill you, but don't tempt me." Polly lowered the rifle to point it at Growcott's legs. "But I can take out a kneecap and then you won't be able to do anything. Think you can get away when you're been shot twice?"

Growcott's breathing was getting so erratic that Morgan was surprised he didn't drop down dead. The big man started to get to his feet, causing Morgan to back up. He didn't want to get into a fight with this man. Even wounded, Growcott was a lot bigger than him and desperate men, like desperate animals, could be dangerous. Fighting was only going to make things worse.

Then Growcott stopped and turned towards Polly. He swayed on his feet, his head starting to loll on his shoulders. Before either Morgan or Polly could get to him, Growcott toppled forward, falling face-first onto the ground with a loud thud. He didn't move.

Morgan hurried to his side and checked for a pulse. It was thready, but it was there, and Growcott was breathing.

Polly lowered the rifle. "Is he alive?"

"Yes, just." Morgan shoved his pistol into his holster. "Go and get the horses. We're going to need to get him back to town before he bleeds out."

"All right." Polly hesitated. "What about you? What if he comes around?"

"I think I can handle it." Morgan shot her a slight smile. "Don't worry about me. Just be quick. I don't want us hanging around here longer than necessary."

Polly looked frozen to the spot. Then she swallowed and nodded, hurrying back along the bank.

Polly sat outside the surgery. She was too exhausted to care that people were walking past her looking at her oddly. Though she was vaguely aware that she didn't look good, dusty and unkempt, with her hair coming out of its braid and wearing clothes not becoming of a woman. Right now, she was having enough trouble keeping her eyes open.

How did Morgan manage to do this every time he went out after a fugitive? It was mentally exhausting, and Polly's body was already screaming at her. She had only done it once, and she was determined that she would never be that stupid and go after someone like that again. But she could certainly appreciate what Morgan had to deal with.

And he had dealt with it brilliantly. Once Growcott had been tied up and put onto the back of Morgan's horse like a sack of potatoes, they had headed back to town. It had taken all day and it was nearly nightfall when they finally arrived back in Jefferson City. Polly was so tired she had almost fallen out of the saddle. Growcott had woken up a few times, only to thrash about and yell as he tried to get out of his bindings. This had caused Morgan's horse to get a little skittish, but by the time they were back on familiar ground, the horse was barely twitching an ear to the tantrums.

Now Growcott was inside the surgery and the shouting had finally stopped. Polly wondered if someone had put a pillow over his face to shut him up. But that was wishful thinking.

As she sat there, staring into the distance, Polly made a promise to herself. When someone said something was too dangerous and she needed to let those who did it for a job handle it, she was going to listen. She wasn't going to let her pride get the better of her or her temper. For a while at least, she was going to do as she was told.

"Polly?"

Polly looked up. Morgan was standing beside her.

"How's Growcott?" she asked.

"He's out now." Morgan made a face as he settled on the sidewalk beside her. "Ernest did his best treating his wrist while Growcott was conscious, but he was fighting back screaming that we were going to kill him. We had to hold him down until the sedative kicked in."

"I wondered why it was so quiet now." Polly yawned and rubbed at her eyes. "It's a pity we can't leave him to rot out there for the wolves and mountain lions."

"We're not savages, Polly." Morgan rubbed his hands over his face. "Once he's cleaned up, we'll charge him with attempted kidnapping and attempted murder of a lawman. Then he'll be taken to Kansas."

"Why Kansas?"

"That's where the bigger jail is. And I don't think Amy would want her father close by, even if he can't go anywhere near her. Once he's served his time, he'll be sent back to where he came from."

"And what if he comes back?"

"Then he'll be run out of town." Morgan glanced at her. "We look after our own here."

Plus, there was a good chance that Growcott would still try to snatch his daughter to use for his own means. Even if Amy was married by that time, he would still attempt to kidnap her. Polly knew there was a chance that he wouldn't let that go. Amy would be relieved that her future family was going to look out for her.

Future family. Did that mean her future family as well? Polly didn't know. She knew what she wanted, but would Morgan want the same thing? One kiss didn't mean anything, and Morgan hadn't brought it up.

"At least it's all cleared up now," Morgan went on. "Chris is going to live, Amy doesn't need to go home, and my brother gets the girl he wants. We all win."

"We all win," Polly murmured. Did they? She didn't feel like she was winning right now. It could be the exhaustion talking, but until Morgan said something about what had happened, they were at an impasse.

It was hard being in love with someone who was so resistant to it.

"We certainly all win." Morgan hesitated. Then he took Polly's hand in his. "I think I win as well."

Was he trying to say...? Polly liked to think she was a forthright person. She liked to speak plainly, but that meant she wanted it in return. Morgan knew that. She shifted so she was facing him, not wanting to pull away from his hand gently wrapped around hers.

"You'll have to let me know what you mean by that. You got the man, is that what you consider winning."

Morgan arched an eyebrow and there was a slight smile twitch of his lips. "You're not going to make this easy for me, are you?"

"You should know me by now. I'm not an easy person."

"That's one of the words I would describe you as." Morgan sighed. "What do I have to do first?"

"Apologize."

"Apologize? For what?"

Polly giggled. "I'll think of something."

Morgan blinked and stared at her. Then realization dawned and he closed his eyes with a groan.

"You little..."

Polly cut him off by tugging his head down and kissing him. Morgan let out a soft sigh and reached for her, but Polly pulled back, still giggling.

"You're going to have to get used to me teasing you, Morgan. There will be a lot of that in the future."

"Will there?"

Polly nodded. Morgan was still watching her as if he had never seen her before. Then he drew her into his arms and kissed her sweetly and softly before pulling back and tucking her into his side.

"You're a wonder, Polly." He rested his chin on her head. "Infuriating, but a wonder."

"You want me to stop being infuriating?"

"Not a chance." Morgan chuckled. "But do you think

you'd be able to manage to be the wife of a US Marshal? I would be gone for weeks at a time, and barely get any time at home. It's unpredictable work."

Polly smiled and looked up at him.

"As you've probably noticed, I'm unpredictable. Besides, I'm sure I can get used to coming along with you if you think you're not tracking criminals as well as you used to."

"You look dead on your feet after just doing it once."

"I'm sure if it meant spending time with you, I could get used to it.

And she would. Even if Polly was completely worn out at the end of the day, she would follow Morgan just to be with him. She could hold her own, he knew that. It wouldn't be too much of a problem.

Morgan arched an eyebrow as he regarded her. Then he groaned and shook his head, pressing a kiss to her forehead.

"I never thought I'd fall in love with such a frustrating woman."

Polly's heart lightened when she heard that. She tugged his head down for another kiss.

"I always knew I'd fall in love with a stubborn man. My mind is pretty set on these things."

"I've noticed." Morgan chuckled. Then he rose to his feet, tugging Polly up with him. "Let's go and get something to eat. I'm starving. And we do have a lot to talk about."

"It sounds good," she said and took his arm. "I love Christmas, do you?"

"I guess as a man I never really took much notice of it."

"Well, that will have to change. I love it, but at home there was never much to celebrate."

Morgan stopped in front of her and looked down at her. "That changes from now on. We will have the most fabulous Christmas you can imagine."

"I like the sound of that," she said as he offered her his arm and they walked down the street.

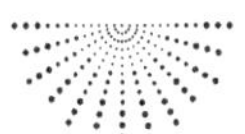

CHAPTER NINE

Pastor Thomas felt his heart a little lighter. Polly was safe and well. He had just seen her in the restaurant down the street with Morgan Foster. Both of them looked worn out but they were smiling as they sat across from each other. As Thomas had watched, Morgan had taken Polly's hand and kissed it. It seemed they did more than hunt Dominic Growcott out in the wilderness. The love in their eyes was plain for all to see.

Thomas couldn't wait to tell Polly's sister, Tracy. She would be relieved and delighted about this. Thomas was, as well. It looked like another one of the Foster brothers would be wed.

The threat Mayor Foster had given him was still on

his mind, and the deadline was looming. Thomas was sure that he would be leaving in a few weeks. Mayor Foster always followed through on his threats and three of the brothers were still resisting their brides. A pain seared through his chest. Tracy was one of those brides and Thomas knew he loved her already. What could he do? If he left and took her with him, he had nothing. Would she even come? If he stayed here, he might have to marry her to another?

If he failed in his task of getting the brothers married and the mayor forced him out... then he wouldn't be able to see Tracy again, not if Mayor Foster blocked him from coming back.

Why are you more concerned about Tracy? You know she's not yours.

I wish she was.

The moment Thomas had accepted that his feelings for Tracy were deepening, he should have distanced himself from her. He had brought her to Jefferson City for a match with a Foster, not with him. And why would she want to be married to a poor pastor? He should have told her to live her own life and limited their contact. But he couldn't. For the first time in his life, Thomas wanted to be selfish and keep the woman he had fallen in love with close.

It was going to be painful to finally marry her to someone. And marry she would. Tracy was a beautiful woman, and men had been approaching her over the last six months to ask to court her. However, Tracy had turned them all away. Thomas couldn't help but be glad about that. However, he knew it wouldn't last forever, and these men had better prospects than he did.

It was painful to admit, but that's how it was.

Thomas arrived back at his home and went inside. Tracy cleaned his house, but she often stayed on to help him out with some of his papers. She had a level head and was better with paperwork than he was. The woman was a miracle, even if they were pushing it by letting her stay longer in his house alone.

Tracy was in his study, sitting behind his desk working on his ledger. She looked up as Thomas came in.

"Pastor Tom." She lowered her pen. "What is it?"

"I've just seen your sister."

"What?" Tracy shot to her feet. "Is she all right?"

"She's fine. Morgan Foster is with her right now. She's safe now and Growcott is in custody."

Tracy whimpered. She pressed a hand to her chest and took a deep breath, letting it out slowly.

"Thank the Lord for answering my prayers. I was really scared."

"She's tougher than you think."

"And impulsive. She makes me want to tear my hair out at times."

Thomas smiled. Of what he knew of Polly Brown, he was not surprised.

"Well, you don't need to do that anymore. She's back and she's safe with Morgan. He won't let anything happen to her."

Thomas hadn't seen Morgan around a woman or pay so much attention to one like Polly, but he knew Morgan's persona. When he was focused on a woman, he gave them his full attention. He was not one to do things by halves. The man was intense, but he was someone Polly could handle. Their interactions over recent months showed they could keep each other on their toes.

That was something of a relief, certainly. All of the Foster brothers were tough, stubborn men. Morgan was the toughest of the lot.

Tracy opened her mouth to say something when there was a knock at the door. A moment later, the knocking became incessant banging. Thomas sighed and headed to the door. His parishioners were not restricted from coming to his home if they needed guidance on anything, but he knew that knocking. It couldn't be anyone else at his front door at night.

He went out into the hall and saw the familiar shape through the faded glass. Thomas had hoped not to see this man until Christmas, at the very least. Any contact with Mayor Foster was a bad thing, although Foster didn't seem to appear to feel the same way.

Crossing the hall, Thomas opened the door. And was almost knocked off his feet as Foster came striding in.

"There's a potential third marriage going to happen soon."

Thomas sighed. As the months had gone on, Foster had become more and more insistent that Thomas should push things along. Thomas knew better than to do that, and it was giving him a headache when Foster tried to push him along. He stayed by the door, keeping it open. Hopefully, he could get Foster to leave within minutes.

"So I've heard, yes. Although, I don't think Morgan's proposed to Polly."

"Oh, there will be a proposal if he knows what's good for him." Foster looked Thomas up and down. "At least your choices haven't proven fruitless. You're slowly getting there."

There was a movement in the hall, and Thomas saw Tracy step out from the study. Her face paled when she saw Foster, but she seemed to be frozen to the spot. Foster frowned when he turned and saw Tracy.

"Miss Brown? What are you doing here?"

"Miss Brown is my housekeeper, Mayor," Thomas said hurriedly. "She was just finishing off some things."

"Oh, was she?" Foster sneered. He glowered at

Thomas. "She's supposed to be making one of my boys fall for her, not working for you. Who's going to see her when she's in here?"

"I'm not about to force one of your sons into anything, Mayor Foster," Tracy said coolly.

"Did I ask you to comment?"

Tracy's face went white, but this time with anger. Thomas was surprised at this change. He had seen Tracy interact with Foster briefly before, and she always seemed to come away frustrated and upset. There was clearly no love lost between them, although from the way Foster was looking at her, his feelings had clearly changed. And it was clear that Tracy knew and she didn't like it.

Thomas didn't like it, either; the man was almost leering.

"You know how hard-headed your sons are. You can't force them into marriage," Thomas said quickly letting a little of his anger loose in his voice.

"I can and I will." Foster declared. "They're my children, so I get to do what I want with them. And I want them all to marry."

"They're grown men, not little boys."

"But they're falling into line now, as I knew they would. You just need to get the other three engaged by Christmas." Foster sniffed and folded his arms. "I'll accept engagements if there isn't a wedding, but if any of them are not engaged by Christmas Day, you can be prepared to leave at New Year."

There it was again. The reason Thomas was doing this in the first place. If it had been anyone else doing this, Thomas would have scoffed and told them to go away. But Mayor Foster was something else entirely. He could easily make sure that Thomas lost his job as the pastor and was driven out of town. It just needed a few whispers in the right ear and then falsehoods would spread so fast that Thomas's head would spin. Falsehoods were far more interesting than the truth, and often more believed. The townspeople of Jefferson City were lovely, but there would always be that doubt about Thomas. He didn't want to go through that; his parents and grandparents had struggled with it when they had helped out those in need, even slaves. Thomas had thought this wouldn't happen to him but it was about to happen, and soon.

"Is this how you treat people who are trying to do a job just so you can get your own way?" Tracy asked hotly. "You want him to fail."

Foster swung around on her.

"If you want to stay here as a 'housekeeper', I suggest you keep quiet. Mind you," he leered at her, which made Tracy step back, "I like a bit of fire. It makes life more interesting. If my boys don't choose you, maybe another Foster will."

Tracy's jaw tightened. Thomas was surprised she didn't bare her teeth.

"I have no desire to marry a Foster."

"We'll see about that." Foster looked her up and down again before turning away. "Remember our agreement, Pastor. You know what I can do if I don't get what I want."

Thomas was still staring after him as the man swept out of his house. Sometimes, it was like dealing with a child about to have a tantrum because he wasn't given his favorite treat for dessert. It was bizarre, particularly with Foster being a grown man. He couldn't really think he could get his sons married in one go, could he?

Oh, he did. Once he set his mind to it, everything went his way or he made everyone pay. Thomas was right in the firing line.

He was beginning to wish he had been brave enough to tell the man no. Then he wouldn't be in this position now.

Then Foster was gone and Tracy closed the door. She looked so beautiful standing there, a glow of anger on her cheeks, her eyes wide and defiant and her head held high. No, he wouldn't have missed this for the world. He just hoped that he could come out of it with his heart intact and Tracy safe and happy.

We hope you enjoyed this story read on for a preview of the next brother's story. Will he find a wonderful new love or will danger and a fugitive take it all away before he can admit his feelings? Read on to find out.

Did you miss book 1, Nicola? Grab it here

"Adam?"

Adam looked up. A tall man wearing a black suit with a black felt hat practically filled the doorway. It looked like he hadn't shaved in a while, judging by the stubble across his jaw. Adam hadn't seen the man look so unkempt before. He put his pen down and stood up.

"Pastor Tom, good afternoon."

"Afternoon." Thomas Brooks started coughing, slapping at his chest as he tried to hold the cough back. "Sorry about that. My chest feels like it's burning right now. Only the Lord knows what I've done to it."

"Maybe head over to Ernest and see if he'll take a look."

Thomas grunted. "I'm sure it's fine. If it's not any better tomorrow, I'll go see him."

Adam resisted the urge to roll his eyes. Pastor Thomas Brooks was one of those people who did his best for everyone else but when it came to looking out for himself he was stubborn and fiercely independent. His energy went towards others instead of his own health. Adam had seen the man do his sermons with pneumonia several times since Thomas had come to Jefferson City, and the women would flock around him to fuss like mad animals. Thomas simply sent them away, refusing to let anyone look after him.

Then again, Thomas had been avoiding Ernest for several months. Adam knew why and understood Thomas's nervousness about seeing the Foster brother who was the most vocal about his father using the pastor to find wives for them. Ernest had declared that it would never happen, and he was not going to fall for it. Judging by the way he acted around the local tribal healer, a beautiful woman called Jacira who worked at the surgery, Adam could understand why he was so upset.

Adam and his brothers did not have the luxury of finding a woman locally. As much as he hated to admit it, women were in short supply in Jefferson City. They were married or too old or too young. What he had to decide was did he want a wife enough to give in to his father?

"Adam?"

Adam blinked. Thomas was now looking at him strangely. Adam cleared his throat and managed a smile.

"Sorry, my mind's still on work." He lied. "How can I help?"

"I understand the mail came in? You sent a message saying I had a few things."

"Oh, right."

Adam went into the storage room behind his desk. His stagecoach company doubled as the post office for packages, and his drivers would do some courier work from time to time. It brought in a little extra cash. Adam made more than enough to live on comfortably, having taken over a few years before from his uncle after said uncle had a bout of poor health. The man was only too happy to let his young nephew take charge of the business.

That had been another source of contention with Adam and his father. Arnold Foster hadn't thought Adam was capable of running a big business, saying Adam was too young. At twenty-four, he was considered young to be in charge, but Adam had argued that he could handle it. Four years on, and the business was thriving. Mayor Foster liked to boast about how successful his children were, but he never actually acknowledged the children when they were in the same room.

Not that Adam cared. He preferred to be away from the man.

Rummaging through a few parcels and found the box with Thomas's packages and brought it through to the main office.

"Here we go. I thought it would be best to keep them here instead of at the general store. You know what

Mrs. Keating's like." Adam placed the box on the desk and checked the five packages. "It looks like you're still getting people writing to you for a husband. And they seem to be writing a book while they're at it."

"I know. They seem to think that writing their life story in one go is going to help me find someone." Thomas sighed and his expression flinched as he saw the parcels. "I took the adverts down months ago. I'm not looking for fresh people."

"People will see the adverts further down the line in an old newspaper and think it's still current." Adam shrugged. "Maybe you could do something with it., After all, if they are desperate enough to write... and you know we need good women out here?"

Thomas made a face. "I might need to if I don't achieve what your father wanted."

That did sober Adam a little. Much as he and his brothers were victims of their father's machinations, Thomas was in as much trouble as they were. He was in danger of losing his job if he didn't get all of Foster's children married by Christmas. Foster couldn't get Thomas to lose his job in a typical way, as such, but he could do whatever he could to make sure Thomas didn't stay in his position as the town's pastor for long. He would spread rumors and build hate and the rest would be history. Adam hated his father at that moment.

He was like a child, in a way. If he didn't get his own way, Foster would throw a tantrum. And Thomas was in the firing line.

"Here." Adam handed the parcels over. "There are times when these come in where I'm not sure whether to be amused or annoyed, you know when I remember how this all started." He shrugged and waved his hands as if to indicate the whole mess.

Thomas winced. "That wasn't my intention, Adam. You know what your father's like. I wouldn't be surprised if he put current adverts in himself and put my name on them."

"I wouldn't be surprised, either." Adam leaned against the desk and folded his arms. "He's still trying to force everyone to do his bidding, yet again. Three of my brothers have now agreed to a wedding. It just needs the other three to fall into line."

Adam winced. that made him sound bitter. He was happy that his brothers had found love, but he couldn't forget the circumstances. Their father had, by instructing Thomas, picked out their brides. Adam didn't want to give Foster the satisfaction of lording it over him.

The image of a beautiful coffee-colored woman floated across his mind, and Adam shoved it aside. He was not going to think about her. Not now.

"Adam, please." Thomas was shuffling from foot to foot. "I'm in an uncomfortable position myself…"

"You could've said no."

"I did. It was only then that he threatened me but worse he threatened to get someone else to do it. You know him… the next person would have cared nothing for the women. They would care nothing for you. I carefully matched the women to each of you and I promised to find them a husband or secure future, if these marriages fell through. Yes, I cared about my job, I love it here but I cared about the women just as much. I even prayed on it and I feel I made the right decision." Now the pastor looked embarrassed. "I've done the best I can for everyone involved. I'm not about to wait around and find out if he can follow through on his threat to make sure I'm run out of town."

"Everyone loves you. Especially the ladies." Adam bit back a laugh as Thomas blushed. "Nobody is going to run you out."

"This is your father we're talking about, Adam."

"Fair point. But he's a fool and behaving like a child."

Adam had been saying that for years. The only reason he and his brothers had remained in contact with Foster was that their mother was still alive, and the six children adored their mother. But when she died, everything was off the table. None of them wanted a relationship with a man who was constantly trying to control them, molding them into people they despised. Foster couldn't see it, he thought he was the epitome of a perfect gentleman. Few if anyone agreed with him, they just went along as he was so powerful.

If they didn't have established lives in Jefferson City, all of the Foster brothers would have moved out of town as soon as they could. Essentially, Morgan as a

US Marshal, could leave and move elsewhere, but the eldest Foster brother saw it as his duty to be the father figure the others needed and so he stayed around. Within reason, considering his job took him all over the place.

It was difficult to try and get on with life when the mayor of the town was their father. To Adam, it felt like he was breathing down their necks all the time.

"Can I ask you a question, Adam?" Thomas asked. "It's about your father, so you can say no… if you want."

"Depends on what you want to ask."

"Why does Foster want everyone married and to have Christmas weddings? That's a rather odd obsession for him."

Adam sighed.

"He and Mother were married on Christmas Day forty years ago this year. Apparently, Father's loved Christmas since he was a small boy. It was the one time in the year when we saw him let his guard down and be the father that we all wanted."

"Do you enjoy Christmas?"

Adam waggled a hand. "I have moments. I enjoyed Christmas as a child, but I knew the next day wouldn't be the same and Father would be back to how he was. Obsessive and controlling, telling us when to sneeze or sit down."

Adam had been five when he first realized that it was not right.

"Can't he be a decent man for the rest of the time?"

"If he is, we haven't seen it. And to have all of us marry on the same day, especially after what happened last year with Chris? That's not right."

It was going to be a bittersweet day for Chris, certainly. Exactly a year since he was left at the altar. His brother was becoming more and more in a bad mood, and that had nothing to do with the fact he had been stabbed and was trying to recover.

"Well, three of your brothers don't seem to be too bothered anymore," Thomas pointed out.

Adam snorted. "It may happen for Matt, James, and Morgan, but I doubt it will for me."

"Oh?" Thomas tilted his head to the side with a slight twitch of an eyebrow. "I'm sure Miss Brough will be happy to hear that."

Adam stiffened. Why did he have to mention her now? He gritted his teeth as a knot built in his belly. "Don't stick me in with Miss Brough, Pastor. She and I are friends, and that's it." He shot Thomas a sly smirk. "Much like you and Miss Brown are friends."

That had Thomas's growing smile disappearing immediately and a slight blush came over his fair complexion.

"Don't start that, Adam. This isn't about me."

"Well, you started it all. You brought them here." Adam chuckled. "I thought you were supposed to pair the ladies off with us, not take one for yourself."

I hope you enjoyed this brief preview of Shelley in this much loved new series. If you are on our newsletter we will let you know as soon as the books are available, if not join here

In the meantime have you read our latest Christmas Box Set? Grab it here

God bless,

Indiana Wake